Pages

A Love Story

Jewel Adams

Jewel Adams

Pages

A Love Story

Jewel Adams

Jewel Adams

Copyright © 2015, 2020 Jewel Adams
Jewel of the West Publishing
All Rights Reserved
ISBN-13: 978-0692415412
ISBN-10: 0692415416

Twilight and evening bell,
And after that the dark!
And may there be no sadness of farewell,
When I embark;
Alfred Lord Tennyson

One of the great truths in life is this: When it comes to love, there is no rhyme or reason and love is never planned. It just happens. It just is.

Joy and pain, wonder, beauty, ecstasy, tenderness, completeness, hurt and healing, a feeling of being whole. Being in love–truly being in love–encompasses all these things.

Or so I have heard.

Jewel Adams

The sea air is cool but comfortable as we walk up the long ramp to board the ship. My sister Anna and her husband Chad have been going on the same Mexican cruise for the past six years now. A few years ago, they invited me to come along to celebrate my thirtieth birthday. I turn thirty-three tomorrow and this will be my fourth cruise with them. At first, I felt like a third wheel, like an intruder. But Anna and Chad quickly put me at ease and I allowed myself to enjoy the trip. Now cruising is one of my favorite vacations.

I have never been married, not even close, and meeting someone on a cruise has never been my goal, though my sister and brother-in-law would not object to companionship for me. Their encouragement is always appreciated, but their subtle attempts at matchmaking go unheeded. Their *Love Boat* plans never pan out anyway. The whole, *"I don't drink or smoke or have sex outside of marriage"* can throw some men off.

Besides, deep inside me lies a secret that I have never told another soul.

You see, on that first cruise, not only did I make a friend, I also lost my heart. The recipient is someone that my sister would least expect, and the person has absolutely no clue he is the keeper of it. He probably never will.

While we wait for our luggage to be taken to our rooms, we grab something to eat at the grill by the pool, which is quickly filling with bikini-clad women and a few generously-tattooed men. The hot tub is occupied as well. Glancing at them,

I think about the one-piece swimsuit I packed and wonder if it will finally see some sun. It has been four years and I have yet to take the price tag off. It's not that I am ashamed of my body. On the contrary, I am very comfortable in my skin and happy with my five-foot-nine curvy figure. But I have always been a private person when it comes to my body and I never flaunt. Of course, I don't dress like a nun either.

By the time we are finished eating (Chad is digesting and preparing for the dinner round) we head to our rooms and find our luggage waiting outside the doors. We always splurge and book suites. There is no way I can stay in a cabin without a window, and the balcony, as well as the roomier interior, are a bonus.

"We're going back up to the pool in a bit," Anna tells me before going into their room. "We will meet up with you later to go to dinner, okay?"

"Sounds good." I appreciate that they know my routine and give me my space.

After unpacking and putting my things away, I walk around the ship for a while and browse the shop windows for a bit before finding a semi-quiet spot to sit until it is time for the mandatory safety drill. This ship isn't too different from its sister ships and I have come to know the layout well.

Planting myself in a deck chair, I use this time alone to think.

To think about *him*.

Changing into a lacy maxi dress, I pin some of my long braids up in a bun with a pair of shiny, black, floral chopsticks, leaving the rest to hang down my back. I quickly apply some lip gloss and spritz on some perfume, then I study my reflection for a moment before grabbing my room key and leaving to meet Anna and Chad.

We are scheduled for the six o'clock dinner seating in the formal dining room. Though most guests are wearing the same clothes they boarded in, I have always liked changing for dinner, just to feel a little special. Well, it may have started out that way, but now . . .

Anna and Chad walk up just as the host crew begin seating. We know the dining area well because Anna usually requests our head server ahead of time to make sure we are seated in his section. I don't know how she manages it, but she does.

"Hello!" Lee says jubilantly. "How are you, my friends?"

"Hi, Lee!" Anna says, hugging him, followed by Chad.

When it is my turn, his smile is wider, his embrace a little longer. "It's good to see you," I tell him.

"It is good to see you, Masai." His voice is soft, his brown eyes filled with their usual warmth.

We take our seats and Lee introduces the two servers assisting him. One of them places our napkins on our laps and hands us a menu while the other places a basket of bread on the table. Lee fills our water glasses. As usual, we are seated at a table for four instead of sharing one of the large round ones that seated bigger groups.

"How have you been, Lee?" Chad asks.

"I have been good. Life is still the same. Nothing changes."

"I don't know how you handle such a grueling schedule," Anna says.

"Been doing it for so long, it is life. I am used to it. How have you all been?"

As the three continue to chat, my mind drifts.

Lee Baitan. After my first cruise, I looked up the meaning of his last name and found out it means goodness. Yes, it was a random thing to do, but the meaning is very fitting.

Lee was born and raised in the Philippines. He had only been married to his wife for less than a year when she passed away from botulism. It happened ten years ago while he was away working on a cruise ship. They had no children, and for many years, Lee harbored deep guilt because he had not been there for his wife. He is an only child and his parents now live in the United States. In fact, this past January they moved from Lansing, Michigan to Provo, Utah.

He was raised a Buddhist, but he and his parents are now Christians, having joined The Church of Jesus Christ of Latter-day Saints nine years ago, something that Lee and I have in common. Living his faith on a cruise ship is difficult, and though he manages, it has troubled him for a long time now.

I learned many of these things through his emails. Emails that I never told anyone I received. Emails that I still receive every month.

As Anna and Chad give one of the assistant servers their order, I discreetly watch Lee greeting another table.

At forty years old, Lee is not what the world would consider very handsome in the conventional sense. Standing a couple of inches shorter than me, he is lean and muscular. His full head of black hair is balding a little in the back and his face bears the typical Filipino features. His wide eyes are framed by thick dark lashes and his lips are full and perfectly shaped. No, he may not be drop dead gorgeous in the worldly way, but when he smiles, his eyes sparkle and his face lights up the room, and he is beautiful to me.

"Your order," the server–Norwood is his name–repeats. Embarrassed, and hoping he hadn't noticed where my gaze had been fixed, I give him my order.

Dinnertime is always my favorite part of the cruise, but not for the food. Sure, the food is wonderful, but food is nothing when Lee is at our table. When he is here laughing and joking with us, I taste nothing. I cherish these times, as well as the few moments here and there that I see him during the cruise, and especially the moments after his shift. Though Lee is considered part of the kitchen crew, his friendships through the years with high-ranking crew members has had its privileges. His position on this ship is as permanent as he wants it to be, his years with the company earning him his own stateroom below when most have to share with a roommate.

Chad had not been exaggerating when he said Lee's schedule is grueling. Most of the cruise ship workers work seven days a week from early morning until late at night, having just enough time to sleep and maybe do a batch of laundry and write an email or two. Lee is usually in the formal restaurant in the mornings and evenings, though it is nearly impossible to see him in the mornings. During lunch he helps out in the buffet restaurant. The workers keep this schedule for ten months out of the year. They are off for the other two and usually go back home to their families. I honestly don't know how they do it. But as Lee said, they get used to it. And I treasure the few stolen moments I get to speak with him.

And they *are* indeed stolen, because it is, after all, against the rules for the crew to mingle with the guests.

When we have finished our appetizer and main course, I order my usual, the signature chocolate melting cake with a scoop of ice-cream, and as usual, Lee is there to serve me, adding an additional scoop of ice-cream because he knows how much I love it. I savor the combined flavor of the creamy chocolate and the vanilla ice-cream, and I thank him again for always taking care of me.

All too soon, dinner is over and it is time for us to leave so we can make it to the early variety show. We tell Lee and his assistants how much we enjoyed the meal and thank him for serving us, to which he always responds, "You will always be my favorite guests and I consider you family." Then we hug him and say we will see him tomorrow. I try to disguise the longing in my gaze. The last thing I want to do is ruin a perfect friendship by giving away how far I have crossed over the emotion line.

He smiles. "I will see you."

The variety show is a tribute to Motown.

The talent is good, and for a short while I am taken back to my childhood when Mama would play old Commodores, Diana Ross, Donna Summer, and Michael Jackson cassette tapes. She would teach Anna and I dances that she and Daddy knew. We knew more 70s music than most of the kids our age in my neighborhood. But I grew to love more than just Motown. Many a night I fell asleep listening to the Bee Gees, Bread, James Taylor, Barbara Streisand, England Dan and John Ford

Coley, and Barry Manilow. I have always loved the classics.

As soon as Barry Manilow enters my thoughts, the lyrics to *Weekend in New England* fill my mind. I have always thought it a sad song, and when I was a teenager it would make me cry, but I still loved it. I still *do* love it. The song is about saying goodbye to someone you desperately love and longing to be with them again. It is about living for the moment you can see them and touch them again.

And I know the feeling well. For the past three years, I have lived all year *every year* to see Lee again, to talk to him and feel his embrace. The friendly hugs and his emails always carry me through to the next year. I admit that I am a sad case, because I know nothing will ever change. Lee will always work the cruise ship. It is his career. I am just a woman who was lucky enough to sit at his table and become his friend.

Lost in the memories of my moments with Lee, my mind drifts back to one memory in particular.

One year, Lee got to spend an hour on Catalina Island, and for half that hour, we sat on a bench and just talked. Because of the crew/passenger rules, I couldn't sit as close to him as I would have liked, but just being with him, soaking in the morning sunshine as the sound of the waves lapped the shore, was enough.

Two years ago.

"You are probably looking forward to your upcoming vacation," I said.

"I am."

"Got any big plans?"

"Not really, just spending some time with my parents." His expression was thoughtful. "More than anything, I look forward to attending church."

"I can't begin to imagine how hard it must be for you, only being able to attend Sunday meetings two months out of the year. That would be so hard. But I am sure the members are glad to have you there when you are."

"I think so. When I am home, my mother and I usually attend the temple once a week."

"That's great. I attend weekly, too."

"Really?"

I nodded. "My week doesn't feel complete without it." I smiled, watching the way the wind ruffled his hair. He was wearing a yellow polo and jeans and I loved seeing him in civilian attire. "Of course, I miss a week whenever I come on a cruise."

His smile widened. "I am glad that you come, and I am sure God understands." Then his expression sobered. "Maybe one day I will have the good fortune of attending the temple with you."

"I would like that."

That had been the biggest understatement I had ever spoken. To attend *anything* with Lee would be wonderful. It would be a dream come true.

When the show is over, Anna and Chad turn in for the night because we will be getting up early to take the shuttle boat over to Catalina Island. Instead of going to bed, I take a stroll out on the deck. Taking a seat in one of the vacant areas (everyone is either inside partying or at the pool) I stare up at the full moon for a while and wait, feeling the longing Barry Manilow sang about, allowing it to carry me away for these solitary moments, because in a little while, the longing will need to be locked away again, buried deep, undetectable. I am very good at it. I have had a lot of practice.

"Masai."

I stand as he approaches. "How did you know I would be here?" I teasingly ask.

He chuckles. "I just knew."

I grin, glancing, at my watch. It is almost eleven already. "I guess I lost track of the time."

His mouth curves. "I'm glad."

"I always worry about you needing your sleep."

"A half hour won't matter." He gestures to the chair and I sit back down. He moves another chair closer and sits. I definitely prefer sitting when I am with him, because even though I am wearing a shorter heeled pair of sandals, they still elevate my height slightly. Whenever I am around Lee, I am more conscious of my height, even though he tells me he likes that I am 'statuesque.'

"I am very happy to see you," he says.

"I'm happy to see you too."

He looks out over the water a moment, his gaze serene in the moonlight. He quietly watches the sea and I silently watch him. His eyes finally meet mine again and we begin to talk a little, filling in the parts of our day to day lives that our emails don't. Since our time is short, we don't waste a moment.

"In your last email, you said you quit your receptionist job and are doing photography full time. I am happy you can now do what you love."

"Me too. It took a while, but now that my portfolio is sufficient, the jobs are steady and I set my own schedule. It has been fun."

"Good. It is important to enjoy your job."

"You should know, Mr. Head Waiter," I say, grinning and he laughs. "You have a great career."

"I do," he agrees, pressing his hands together. I watch the veins move beneath his skin. "Can't beat the benefits and the perks."

"I'm sure."

I wonder if it is just my imagination or if he is a little somber tonight. I decide he is probably just tired.

When he grows quiet again, I stand. "We should probably go. We both have to get up early and I don't want to keep you from getting the sleep you need."

He stands as well, surprising me by reaching for my hand. Lacing his fingers through mine, he says, "Tomorrow is your birthday. I have something for you."

"Really? You don't need to give me anything."

Squeezing my hand gently, he releases it and softly brushes his fingers against my face before lightly cupping my cheek. For a moment, I forget to breathe. "Meet me here tomorrow night. Please. I will come as soon as I can."

I have never seen his eyes so imploring. I would do anything for him, anything he asked. "I will be here. I promise."

Brushing a thumb over my cheek a final time, he nods and walks away.

After a night of very little sleep, I wander in and out of various Catalina shops with Anna and Chad. When Anna comments on me dragging this morning and asks if I am okay, I assure her that I am fine, just a little tired.

"I'm glad it's not a migraine," Anna says and I can hear the concern in her voice. She remembers all too well the debilitating migraines I used to get, especially when I was sleep-deprived the night before. I used to run on three, sometimes four hours of sleep a night because of insomnia.

Now, thanks to large doses of melatonin and valerian, I usually get a good night's sleep. Usually. I haven't had a bad one in a long time, but I keep updated prescription pain medication handy just in case.

Wanting to ease her mind, I purposely perk myself up. It is my birthday, and perkiness is expected. It was indeed a long night, the sleepless moments filled with thoughts of Lee, reliving his touch over and over, and asking myself what it all means.

Shaking my head, I focus my thoughts on the present and enjoy my time with my sister and brother-in-law. I purchase a few clothes that I really love and Anna and Chad buy me a gorgeous leather purse for my birthday.

We walk down to the beach and Anna and Chad decide to take off their shoes and wade in the water along the shore. I get out my camera and take a few pictures of them. Anna will most likely frame them when we get back home. She always does. She has never been into scrapbooking. She is into framing, and her family room walls are covered with vacation photos–from vacations they have taken with their three kids to the ones she and Chad have taken alone. There are also, of course, cruise photos of the three of us. I've mentioned frequently that she needs to take up scrapbooking because when the 'Big One' finally hits Salt Lake City, those frames are history. She never appreciates the reminder.

When Chad begins to chase Anna with a big old piece of seaweed, she screams, threatening him at the top of her lungs with all manner of bodily harm, and I am soon laughing so hard, I can't hold the camera still.

"Those two are something else," a masculine voice says.

Chuckling, I turn to him. He is a fellow passenger from the ship. "They are about as crazy as they come," I agree.

"I'm Jake," he says, putting out his hand and I shake it.

"Masai."

"Good to meet you, Masai. That's an interesting name."

"Yeah, well, I have interesting parents, as testified by my crazy sister over there."

He laughs. "Must be a fun family."

"You have no idea."

Shaking his head, he laughs again. "Well, I'm heading back. It's good to meet you. Maybe I'll see you later."

"Good to meet you, too," I say, unwilling to respond to the latter part of the comment and risk offering encouragement. "See ya." I allow my eyes to follow him briefly as he walks away. He is blond, tall and well built. Anna would say he's a hottie because he is her type. Chad is also tall, blond and well built, like Jake.

But Jake is not Lee.

On the way back to the dock to wait for the shuttle, I stop in my favorite little candy shop and purchase some chocolate. I have made a habit of sharing it with Lee sometime during the cruise. He appreciates that I think of him.

When we get back to the ship, I grab a quick lunch at the buffet, smiling at Lee as he helps out behind the line. Most of his dark hair is covered by a paper hat, but I would recognize those eyes and that smile anywhere.

Grinning in return, he says, "Happy Birthday!"

"Thank you."

"Did you have a good morning?"

"I did."

"Did you get chocolate?" His voice is teasing.

"Of course."

After standing there smiling at him a little too long, I tell him, "See you at dinner," and move along to keep from holding up the line, when more than anything, I just want to stay in that spot and not move until he does.

"See you at dinner," he says back and I walk away, briefly catching the smile his co-worker gives him. Taking a seat at the table with Anna and Chad, I eat my small meal, glancing frequently in Lee's direction, and then return to my cabin for a much-needed nap.

At dinner, Lee, Norwood and Liam sing the birthday song to me and I make a wish over a piece of chocolate cake. Of course, Lee brought me two scoops of ice-cream to go with it. I giving him a tender smile, expressing my gratitude for his continued thoughtfulness.

Just then, Jake, the guy I met on Catalina earlier, walks by with another couple.

"Happy Birthday, Masai," he says, stopping at our table. I had not realized he was seated so close. "Why didn't you tell me earlier it was your birthday?"

"Because you were a stranger earlier."

"Well, I'm not now, am I?" His tone is flirty, his smile wide.

I glance at Anna and her smile is just as wide. She gives me a blatant look of encouragement. I also see the questions in her eyes. *Who is he and why did you not tell me you met him?*

I briefly glance up at Lee, but he quickly looks away and begins to clear a few empty dishes from the table.

"Hey," Jake says, "after you're done with dinner, why don't you join us and let us help you celebrate?"

Lee's back is to me and I watch his shoulders stiffen briefly before he walks away, taking dishes to the kitchen. "Thanks, I appreciate the offer, but not tonight."

"Are you sure?" he tries again, slight disappointment in his eyes.

"Yeah, I didn't sleep too well last night and I'm pretty tired."

"Okay, but if you change your mind, we will be in the lounge on the main floor of the atrium."

"Thanks," I tell him, attempting to infuse sincerity into my voice, not the least bit tempted by his offer.

When Jake and his friends leave, I look around for Lee and spot him a few tables away talking with the guests.

"Girl, that man was fine," Anna says. "You should have gone with them and had some fun. I would have if I was single. I mean, he's got it going on and . . ."

"I'm right here, babe," Chad reminds his wife, putting an arm around her and she laughs.

Jewel Adams

"I know." She pats his cheek lovingly. "Just trying to help my sister out. He was fine, but he doesn't have anything on you."

I can't help but smile as I watch them. They are both two years older than me and have been married for twelve years, and I have never seen two happier people. Even when their kids are driving them crazy, they are happy because they have each other.

They have everything I want.

Lee finally returns to our table and I thank him for the wonderful birthday dinner.

"It was so much fun and I really appreciate it," I tell him.

"You are very welcome. I'm happy we could help you celebrate."

"So am I," I say, warmth filling me. I keep my eyes from lingering on him, not wanting Anna to glimpse anything in my expression.

32

We all stand to leave. Again, his embrace is warm and his arms are home, but this time it is physically painful to move away.

It is because of the touch last night.

His touch against my cheek has weakened me, making it harder to keep my feelings hidden. Still, I try.

Instead of my usual walk afterward, I spend this time on my stateroom balcony, not wanting to risk running into Jake. A little after ten, I make my way out to our meeting spot on deck. There, I wait for Lee.

Jewel Adams

It is almost midnight and he hasn't shown, and I have an overwhelming urge to cry. Thinking about Jake's earlier invitation, I realize Lee had heard him ask me, but he never heard my answer. Does he think I am with Jake? Did he think I changed my mind about meeting him tonight? Did he forget to come? He had to know I would keep my word. His friendship is too important to me to do otherwise.

Or maybe he finally sensed my true feelings for him and decided not to come. I could kick myself for being so transparent!

Angry at myself, I blink the tears away, deciding not to wait any longer. I have lost too much sleep as it is and I will never be able to function tomorrow.

As I stand to leave, suddenly he is here and my heart lightens.

"I'm so sorry, Masai. Tonight, it took a lot longer to close up."

"It's okay." I smile, my gaze dropping to the gift shop bag in his hand.

He hands it to me. "Happy Birthday. I have to go, but thank you for waiting."

Before I can respond, he turns and walks away. I can't fault him. It is so late, he will probably be dragging tomorrow as much as I will, and he can't afford to be tired.

"Goodbye, Lee," I whisper and head back to my room, choosing to wait until I am there to open the bag.

Quickly changing for bed, I say my prayers and pull back the covers, slipping beneath them. Then I open the bag and take out the package. It is wrapped in tissue paper and I tear it open. Inside is a leather-bound journal. It is about five-by-seven and looks very old. I loosen the leather tie and open it.

On the inside of the cover is written:

For you, son.

On these pages, begin your life anew.

Allow the grief to flow and give it passage.

Then forgive yourself and let go.

Record the things here that matter.

I finger the first page. It is covered in gold leaf work. The pages are trimmed in gold and are thin like tissue paper, making the whole book look like an antique. Leaning back against the pillows, I turn the page and begin to read what I assume to be Lee's handwriting.

May 21

Though my father gave me this journal years ago, I had no desire to write in it until now.

Tonight, for the first time in years, my heart smiled.

Her name is Masai. She is the sister of Chad and Anna, two repeat guests that I have come to think on as friends, and she is the most beautiful thing I have ever seen. She is tall, a couple of inches taller than me, with rich caramel skin, long dark braids, and a Marilyn Monroe figure, the kind that has always appealed to me. But it was not those things that captured me. It was her spirit, an ingrained kindness that radiated from her, immediately touching me. For the first time in my life, I was instantly drawn to someone.

How can this be?

It seems I am not dead inside after all.

~This past month has been one of pondering. I have some decisions to make. I just need to be brave enough to make them.

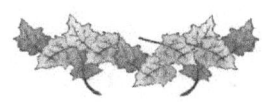

May 22

I glimpsed Masai today at the lunch buffet. She did not see me.

Tonight, I discovered that her birthday was two days ago and this trip is a present from Anna and Chad. She ordered chocolate melting cake for dessert and I added an extra scoop of ice-cream, wishing her a happy birthday as I served her. She joked with me about knowing the way to her heart. I discovered through the meal that she has a great sense of humor. Like many guests, she asked me about myself. I answered her questions, leaving out the details I do not normally share with people I don't know. She looked so beautiful in her black formal gown. It was modest, but it still loosely hugged her curves, befitting a woman of virtue, for that is how I see her.

When I finished my shift, I saw Masai again. She was out walking. She told me insomnia keeps her awake so she never goes to bed until almost eleven. She was heading up to walk on the deck for a few minutes, and before I could stop to think of my actions, I was walking with her. We talked and I found myself sharing a few details of my life with her. We talked about my career choice, the pros and cons.

I told her of Lana's death. She is a good listener, full of so much empathy and compassion, I could not help but open to her. While we talked, she shared chocolate with me that she bought today on Catalina Island.

I know after tonight her friendship will be a treasure to me, one that I will do my best to never lose.

May 23

Today Masai spent the day in Ensenada with her family, so I did not see her until dinner. The Mexican sun bronzed her skin, giving her a glow. If it is possible, she is even more beautiful. I took her order first and served her meal first. I did this without thinking. I don't know what that means.

Tonight, after the variety show, she came back by to say thank you again. I asked her if she would be out walking and she said she would. I met her by the pool and we visited for a few minutes, talking of everything and nothing. Then we said goodnight.

May 24
Sea Day

I glimpsed her again at lunch today. It is frustrating being unable to go to her, to talk with her.

Tonight, at dinner, I brought her three scoops of ice-cream with her melting cake. The scoops really are not that big anyway.

Later when we talked, we discovered a common bond. She is of my faith. I could not believe it. It really should not have been a surprise. The light of Christ shines within her. It shines through her eyes. It has since the moment I met her.

Saying goodbye was more complicated than it should have been. It hurt like hell. We exchanged email addresses and I promised to keep in touch.

I don't like goodbyes.

May 25
Tonight, I walked the deck alone.

May 26
Starting tonight, the time I would have spent with Masai will be spent in prayer and study.

I need the blessings.
I also still need to make a choice.

I cannot believe what I have been reading. From the first word, I was captivated, entranced. These are Lee's private thoughts–his thoughts about me! What I am glimpsing now in his written words gives new depth to his emails, and they only serve to make me love him even more, if such a thing is possible. It's as if I can suddenly read between the lines, see the things he doesn't say. It makes me wish I had copies of his emails with me now.

I know I need to sleep. I even feel the stirrings of a headache coming on, but I feel compelled to keep reading.

The Next Year

May 15

My heart is full again because Masai came back with her family. I thought I remembered how beautiful she was. I was mistaken. We embraced and all the memories of last year rushed back. They are the only guests that I have ever felt familiar enough with to hug–because they are family to me. I truly realize that now.

Tonight, I was late getting done and we only had a couple of minutes to speak. So, we said nothing. But her beautiful, serene smile said much.

May 16

I was able to go ashore for an hour today. Half that hour was spent sitting on a bench visiting with Masai while Anna and Chad looked at watches in a jewelry store. Sitting in the sun with her was a decadent experience, one that will stay with me forever. We did not talk about anything special and there was nothing new to share. It was her nearness. A full thirty minutes of just being with her was everything. I kept an adequate amount of space between us, just in case another crew member passed and saw us talking. We could not look too familiar.

Tonight, we spoke of the gospel and the miracle of the atonement. And I silently admitted what my heart has known all along.

I love her. So much it hurts.

But I cannot have her.

Because I still haven't chosen.

May 17

Holding so much inside is making my heart ache.

Still, it is a beautiful heartache and I would never wish it away.

I couldn't, because I would rather have the pain and feel the accompanying ecstasy of having her in my life than feel nothing.

May 18

Tonight, when we met, I gave her a card to open on her birthday. I hate that

I will miss it and I wish I could really celebrate it with her. We hugged and said goodbye. I wish I did not have to be away from her.

I wish for so many things . . .

May 19

I am in desperate need of the sacrament.

I am in desperate need of her.

The Next Year

May 22

She is here and I feel alive again.

I have never seen a pair of eyes more beautiful than Masai's when she looks at me.

When she came to dinner, it was hard to conceal the longing I feel for her. The love. And when we met later tonight, it was even more difficult.

Father in Heaven, I don't know what to do anymore.

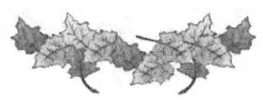

May 23

One of the newer male crew members was caught this morning exiting a guest's room. He will lose his job.

Because of this, I did not meet Masai tonight. I slipped her a note during dinner. I hope she understands.

May 24

I visited with Masai and her family during dinner, but I did not meet her again tonight.

I really miss her, even though she is here.

How can I miss her so much?

May 25

Dinner and brief glimpses are not enough.

They will never be enough.

I die a little more inside each time I have to say goodbye.

And I wonder which goodbye will finally be the last.

There is never a guarantee that there will be a next time.

I need to remember that.

This Year
May 19
Masai is here!

I am happy, but I am in agony because I sense a change in her.

A change I am responsible for.

I have to do something.

May 20
Today was her birthday and we sung to her at dinner. Then a male guest stopped by to talk with her. It was the first time I have ever experienced burning jealousy. I don't like that feeling.

Tonight, I'm giving her a gift.

I'm giving her a part of me.

My heart.

By the time I have finished, I am exhausted, but I also notice something.

Record the things here that matter.

His only entries are when I have been here. *I* am the thing that matters. *Me* and *God*. After all this time, to finally know that I am not alone in my feelings leaves me without words.

After the slow buildup, the pain between my eyes has turned into a full-blown migraine that has become excruciating. Making my way to the vanity, I search my toiletry bag for the pain and nausea meds, grateful that I remembered to bring them. I take a pill from each bottle and get into bed, immediately shutting off the light because light makes the pain worse–that and reading with a headache.

As I have always done, I try to breathe deeply and count in my head for as long as it takes, until the meds finally kick in and I drift off.

Jewel Adams

Lee

Lee has been anxious all day, and tonight as he watches Anna and Chad move through the dining room and approach their table, his heart drops.

Masai is not with them.

He draws forth a wide smile. "Hello, how are you this evening?"

"We're fine," Anna says, her voice lacking its usual enthusiasm.

Where is Masai? "Just you two tonight?"

"I'm afraid so," Chad answers. "Masai has been in bed with a migraine all day."

Because of my journal? "I hope she will be all right," he says, doing his best to ignore Chad's arched brow, knowing he isn't doing too good a job of keeping his feelings hidden. His attempt at schooling his features isn't working well tonight.

"She will," Anna says. "She used to have them all the time, but getting more sleep regularly helped. She hasn't been sleeping well the past few nights, which triggered it again. I'm sure she will be better tomorrow."

She hasn't been getting enough sleep because of me.

Disguising a heavy heart, Lee serves them and takes care of all his guests. Worry for Masai consumes his thoughts the entire shift, but somehow, he makes it through.

When he finally makes it to his cabin, Lee drops to his knees by the bed, praying harder than he ever has before. His prayer is two-fold and he is determined to stay on his knees, no matter how long it takes.

A long while later, he finally goes to bed, his thoughts consumed with the answer the Spirit had whispered with a clarity that cannot be ignored.

Jewel Adams

I sleep in. When I wake to a knock at the door, there is only a dull throbbing in my head. I get up and answer it, knowing it is Anna checking up on me.

"Are you okay?" she asks, worry etching her lovely features. I hate worrying her. "Chad can give you a blessing if you need him to."

"I'm better this morning. I'm going to shower and grab something to eat, maybe lounge in one of the darker areas on the ship so the cabin guy can clean my room."

"Okay. We've eaten already, but I can come up with you if you want."

"No, you and Chad go do whatever you planned to. I'll be fine. After napping today, I'll be ready for our last night."

"Okay, we'll see you later."

Staying ahead of the migraine this time, I take more medication. As I told Anna, I will spend the afternoon napping, because nothing is going to stop me from going to dinner tonight or having my last moments with Lee. Other than a few hazy dreams of the journal pages, I slept soundly. Now that I am awake, all I can think about is what I learned last night reading his thoughts.

Lee loves me. He truly loves me. All this time he has kept his feelings locked away as tightly as I have my own.

But why has he not said anything? Probably for the same reason I haven't. Ours is an impossible situation. But why open to me now? And what happens now?

After showering and dressing, I leave the housekeeping service sign hanging on my door and head up to the buffet to have a quick breakfast. I hadn't expected to see Lee, there, but I am still disappointed when I don't.

Since the library is empty, I sit in one of the corner chairs far away from the windows and rest my head in my hands for a while. When I start feeling too drowsy from the meds, I get up and make my way back to my room, relieved to find it cleaned. I thank Han, the cabin boy, before closing the door and he wishes me a good day.

Waiting in line outside the dining room doors, I am so nervous I can barely breathe. I don't know what I will say to Lee, but I need to tell him how I feel. Tonight, I will. We will make it work somehow. We have to, and I am willing to do whatever it takes.

Taking a deep breath as the line begins to move, I follow Anna and Chad inside.

When Lee's eyes finally meet mine, his mask is lowered and the longing is there for the world to see.

"I am glad you are well, Masai."

"Thank you."

He pulls out my chair, allowing his hand to linger on my shoulder a moment after I am seated.

Lee's tables fill quickly tonight and he is running quite a bit, but he always spares a moment to visit and joke with us before moving to another table. Tonight, I watch him as often as I can.

After one of his stops to check on us, Anna says, "For some reason I am really going to miss him this time," and I silently agree.

"We will miss him too," Norwood says, refilling our water glasses.

"What do you mean?" Chad asks and I silently echo his question.

"He is leaving the cruise line."

"Leaving?" I manage to voice around the ball of emotion lodged in my throat.

"Yes," Norwood says. "His contract is up and he won't be renewing. When he leaves for vacation tomorrow he will not be coming back."

The choice. This was the choice he wrote about in his journal. It had been vague and I couldn't understand. Now I know.

I turn as Lee walks toward our table with a tray of desserts on his shoulder. He places it on the service stand. When he looks at me, tears fill his eyes, and mine. Throwing all reserve to the wind, I stand and he comes to me, taking my hands in his and the rest of the room fades away. He is all I see.

His eyes move over the dining area a moment before returning to me, and in them I can see that he no longer cares about the rules. Then he releases my hands and his arms are around me. I vaguely hear Anna's dramatic gasp and Chad's exclamation of, "I knew it!" Wrapping my arms around his neck, I press a hand into his hair, touch my forehead to his and ask, "Why did you not say anything?"

"I couldn't until I made a choice. And I finally did." His adoring gaze roams over my face. "I choose you. I love you, Masai, and I promise I will always choose you."

He kisses me then, and amid the growing applause and cheers of nearby guests, I lose myself in the warmth of his mouth and the haven of his firm embrace, armed with the knowledge that all my hopes and dreams are finally coming true.

It is one of the happiest moments of my life.

Epilogue

One year later
Bountiful, Utah

Standing in front of the family room fireplace with my hand resting on my seven-month round stomach, I study my weddings rings for a long moment before lifting my gaze to our wedding portrait above the mantle. Beneath it sit several other photos of us that we have taken since then.

We were married in the Bountiful Temple surrounded by my family and his parents. I smile as I remember him telling me over and over throughout that day how beautiful I was, and he still never lets a day pass without telling me. He will definitely always be the most handsome man in the world to me.

We honeymooned in Park City. Lee fell in love with the mountains and neither of us desired a more exotic destination. We'd both had our fill and wanted to be closer to home.

I came to him inexperienced in matters of sexual intimacy, and I found myself grateful for his experience. He was gentle, patient and tender with me, and sharing the sacred act with him was more wonderful than I ever dreamed it would be. I never imagined feeling such closeness, such wonder and passion.

Lee's adjustment to land life was so smooth and fast, it was hard to believe he'd worked on a cruise ship for as long as he had. Because he had saved most of his pay through the years and I had a nice amount put away from abundant photography work, we were able to sell my condo and pay cash for a brand-new starter home without going into debt, and still have a nice cushion in the bank. The furniture from the condo was enough to furnish the whole house so we saved there as well.

Since Lee is fluent in Tagalog, Cantonese and Spanish, he was able to get a translation job at a staffing service in Salt Lake City and he is enjoying it immensely.

Once a month, we drive down to Provo to see his parents. The Baitans are two of the kindest people I know and I always feel welcome there. Lee feels the same when we visit my parents or attend family functions. Mine has become a very diverse family, which thrills my parents because of the eclectic mix of grandchildren they will have, and they happily admit that fact. As Lee has learned, there is definitely no shortage of fun in the Grant family.

Hearing the garage door opening, my heart begins to flutter. Lee is home. It is Saturday and he has been at the church playing basketball with the other elders. He may be shorter than half the priest quorum, but he has one heck of a jump shot. He lands more three pointers than anyone in the group and they love him. And the young men always want to practice with 'the old guy.' He told me he played a lot of basketball when he was younger and he is happy for the chance to be so active in it again.

My husband is sweaty as he pulls me to him, his gray t-shirt damp, but I don't care. He presses his lips to mine, his lean, muscular arms circling my expanded waist.

"Did you win?" I ask him, burying my fingers in his hair.

"We did." He kisses me again with a hint of passion that makes my temperature rise, renewing in me a longing and need for him that will never fade.

"Did you still want to go and buy the extra mulch for the garden?"

"Later," he breathes.

"So, what should we do now?" I ask as his kisses drift to my neck.

"Maybe we should take up where we left off this morning," he murmurs huskily against my skin.

"Maybe we should."

As we head upstairs Lee's cell phone rings and he checks the ID. "It's Chad again, probably calling again about doing another grill off."

"Do you want to call him back?"

He snorts. "Making love to my wife is more important than food."

I laugh. "That's good to know."

* * *

Long after the passion is spent and we are lying in each other's arms, I whisper against his smiling mouth, "Always better than food."

About the Author

J. Adams has written books in different genres, but her main focus is inspirational interracial romance. She is a motivational speaker to both youth and adult audiences. In her spare time (when she has any) you can find her curled up with a good book and a healthy stash of orange Tic Tacs.

She and her family reside in Utah.

Email: jewela40@gmail.com

Website: Angelospromise.weebly.com

& JewelAdams.com
Available at Amazon

www.ingramcontent.com/pod-product-compliance
Lightning Source LLC
Chambersburg PA
CBHW071344130626
46556CB00005B/2017